THE SECRET PLOTS

OF DESTINY

A romantic suspense novel set in Greece, where a mature woman's summer escape turns into a life-changing journey filled with secrets, passion, and unexpected twists.

DANIELA DI DOMENICO

*****

"Looking around" is the watchword for anyone who wants to pursue their own destiny. Even when we repeatedly dwell on the problems that need to be resolved, the traumas and wounds that have been suffered, we must not forget to look beyond, so as not to restrict our life to a continuous struggle aimed at rebalancing a past that no longer exists. Rachele, the protagonist of this story, decides to act rather than be overwhelmed by the anxieties and fears that often cloud the mind, preventing us from seeing other paths that fate might have in store for us.

*****

Contents

Did this story touch your heart?

Join **Daniela Di Domenico's Readers Circle** *and be the first to know when the next tale of secrets and passion arrives.*

Scan the QR *code to stay in touch.*

Chapter One

Rachele woke suddenly and, almost instinctively, found herself standing by the window overlooking the sea. Though it was still the middle of the night, the soft glow from the streetlights revealed the gentle waves softly lapping the shore. She lived in Savona, a city she cherished. To her, it was a sanctuary—peaceful and discreet, reflecting the Ligurian temperament. The sea, with its deep blue hues against the green hills, created an enchanting scene.

For weeks, she had been waking up at around four in the morning, unsettled by a vague sense of unease, a lingering premonition that kept waking her in fits. Rachele, a forty-six-year-old woman, was of average height and slim, with soft chestnut-brown hair that reached her shoulders. She had large, expressive brown eyes and a captivating gaze. She carried herself with confidence, exuding independence and pride, always maintaining a graceful, poised demeanour.

For nearly twenty years, she ran a real estate agency with her close friend Marina. To her, it hardly felt like "work" because it was a passion, something that brought her both joy and a deep sense of satisfaction. Over those two decades, she had dedicated herself to perfecting her skills, driven by a blend of ambition and passion, always seeking to achieve more with greater efficiency. She was dependable and dedicated, a true professional, methodical and composed in everything she did.

After a long and tumultuous eight-year relationship with Giorgio, an architect from Genoa, she chose to live alone again, having accepted that their relationship had come to an end. It took her a while to truly see just how deeply insensitive he was, concealing his true self behind the guise of a perfect gentleman.

In reality, he was a manipulative man, incapable of feeling real emotions. At first, he placed her on a pedestal, and Rachele felt flattered, loved and respected. She had begun to believe she was lucky to have found the perfect man. However, as time passed, things changed drastically. Only afterward did she realise that it had all been part of a diabolical trap designed to bind her ever closer to him, smothering her most intimate passions, such as her love for travel, her dedication to her work, her loyal, cherished friendships, and her dream of having children and a beautiful family, being an only child herself.

Giorgio knew her insecurities and anxieties well, using them to provoke and hurt her. He often started arguments, but before things could spiral, he would offer an excuse, saying, "I'm sorry, I didn't mean it" or "You know I didn't mean what I said...", always making sure she calmed down afterwards. He always managed to convince her that his hurtful words and aggressive actions were never intended to hurt her. Unfortunately, this behaviour became more frequent, and, after reaching her breaking point, she could no longer tolerate it and saw through Giorgio's calculated behaviour, the empty promises meant to deceive, the feigned remorse, and hollow apologies. He always swore he would change, all the while testing her patience and forgiveness.

Every celebration, just like every holiday, was ruined by his arrogance. He was frequently disrespectful towards her, even in front of others. In recent years, he had also tried, unsuccessfully, to isolate her from her friends and family, seeking her complete dependence on him. His possessiveness knew no bounds and he demanded all her attention solely for their relationship.

The last year of living together had been the worst, with Giorgio seizing on her every little mistake and distraction to belittle her and increasingly undermine her self- esteem.

Rachele experienced one of her most humiliating moments at the home of Roberto, a dear friend who ran a real estate agency in Savona. Their friendship was solid, born from working together for over ten years.

Roberto had invited Rachele, Giorgio, and other friends to celebrate his birthday. Among the guests were Daria, the birthday boy's girlfriend, Marina, Rachele's best friend, and an architect named Flavio. Maria, Roberto's sister, was also there with her husband Andrea, both of whom were physiotherapists. Additionally, there were Filippo and Tania, a couple of real estate agents, and finally Stefano and Guglielmo, surveyors who had been Roberto's friends since high school.

The table was laid out beautifully and the evening was pleasant and fun, filled with comical anecdotes shared by those present about various clients, which made everyone laugh. At a certain point, Daria went to the kitchen to get the cake. When she returned to the living room, she placed it on the table. Upon seeing it, everyone began to clap, impressed by the extraordinary design: a beautiful, colourful villa with the words 'Happy Birthday King of Sales' written in chocolate beneath".

Moved and grateful, the birthday boy opened a bottle of champagne, courtesy of Stefano and Guglielmo. He filled everyone's glasses, then expressed his thanks with warmth and affection to those who had made the evening special.

«I would also like to dedicate this toast to my dear friend Rachele», he added, gazing directly into her eyes. «It's true that I've closed many sales this year, but many of them were the result of our teamwork!».

Rachele felt herself blushing, but she raised her glass again, acknowledging his kind words. «To me, in addition to being a great friend...», he continued, «she's also the best real estate agent in Savona, no disrespect to anyone else, of course! She has an amazing knack for business and always manages client relationships brilliantly and with great diplomacy!».

Everyone complimented her... everyone except Giorgio! That toast and, more specifically, those compliments, stirred a blinding envy in him, who, unlike her, was going through a rather difficult time at work. Flushed with anger, he replied loudly, so that everyone could hear: «Roberto, you must have the wrong person!», he sneered, «Rachele the best real estate agent in Savona? Of course not! She's successful at work because of her beautiful body... that's the only reason she manages to trick clients!»

Those words left everyone stunned, especially Rachele, who barely held back tears, feeling deeply humiliated by her own companion, no less, and in front of people who, thankfully, she had known for a long time and who held a completely different opinion of her.

It was Roberto himself who regained control of the situation, defending his friend's ability and worth. He stared at Giorgio with contempt and, without mincing his words, replied that perhaps what he had just said was merely driven by envy.

«She's a truly capable woman and it has nothing to do with the fact that she's also beautiful! I've seen her in action and, believe me, she's the best. You've been her partner for years, so you should know that better than any of us, but from the way you act, it seems you don't understand a thing about her! I would never talk like that about my partner; you probably don't deserve someone like her, and I'm amazed she's still with you!». There were a few tense moments during which Giorgio looked ready to punch Roberto.

However, in the end, it was Daria who restored calm, trying to redirect attention to the celebrations:

«So, who's going to help me cut the cake? I don't want to ruin it!».

That evening left a deep scar on Rachele's heart and she now understood that she no longer had feelings for the man who never missed an opportunity to make her feel like a nobody.

The insults became increasingly vicious, the threats less veiled, because he was no longer able to manipulate her or control her emotions.

Growing more contemptuous and agitated, he denigrated her intelligence, appearance, and behaviour, treating her as if she were a fool.

Giorgio's reactions were always fuelled by a twisted envy, likely because Rachele had a natural way of relating to people that he lacked. She was an excellent communicator, an attentive listener who could connect differently with each person she encountered, skills that made her successful at work.

Giorgio, however, saw everything in black and white, while for Rachele, the world was full of shades and beautiful colours.

Realising that their relationship had irreparably broken down and that nothing remained to be salvaged, she developed a strong need to distance herself from that narcissistic, malignant and sociopathic man.

So, one morning, she left the house they had shared for eight years on the outskirts of Genoa, taking with her a lot of bitterness and few happy memories.

Chapter Two

She had chosen the place where she would live very carefully and, for more than a year, she had settled in Savona, on the Lungomare degli Artisti. She found a small yet charming penthouse of eighty square metres, which she had furnished with immense passion in a country style, where wood was the undisputed protagonist. The beautiful parquet, stained in a pale colour that enhanced the natural grain, made the space warm and welcoming, like a true refuge.

The colours on the walls were strictly pale, pastel shades: the kitchen and living room were light green, while the bedroom and study were ochre yellow. In keeping with the style she had chosen for her new home, all the accessories were made of wood and white ceramic, many of which were decorated by hand. The kitchen had an old, authentic feel, enriched by small pots containing aromatic and fragrant plants: laurel, rosemary, lavender and thyme, placed somewhat randomly on shelves, countertops and windowsills. She used an old wardrobe as a pantry, which she bought in a second-hand furniture store and that a friend had restored.

A distinctive wall open on both sides and covered in white stone separated the kitchen from the living and dining areas. The furniture was rustic yet chic at the same time. Two white cotton sofas, adorned with lobster- coloured cushions, were arranged casually. In front of them was a small solid wood table, also painted white, matching the large rectangular table in the dining area. The space was very bright, thanks also to the large window overlooking the sea.

The bedroom had a unique charm: Rachele had chosen a wrought iron bed with a romantic design, a true work of art, accented with vintage fabrics and lace. Facing the bed was a beautiful, large, cream-coloured wardrobe with a central arch. Hand-painted ceramic lamps contributed beautifully to the room's enchanting atmosphere.

The bathroom, on the other hand, was impeccably white and consistent with the rest of the house, furnished with modern white wooden pieces that made it both inviting and intimate.

The apartment was surrounded by a wonderful, large balcony adorned with ornamental plants and wicker furniture, offering a breathtaking view. She loved looking out over the sea and each day, upon waking, seeing it before her filled her with a sense of serenity and contentment.

Not to mention the promenade below with its mosaics: that was something truly special!

The pavement stretched nearly a kilometre, featuring a blue and white mosaic interspersed with panels depicting sketches by various artists who frequented the town in the '50s and '60s. These panels showcased marvellous works of art, such as *Le Nature* by Lucio Fontana and *Monumento ai Caduti di Tutte le Guerre* by Leoncillo Leonardi.

Every time she walked along the promenade, Rachele was filled with the sensation of being in a real open-air museum. She walked it daily on her way to the office, just a few hundred metres from her home.

She had carefully planned her new life: both her home and work were in strategic, nearby locations. At work, she had started to prioritise stability over anything that might involve risk. When her partner Marina mentioned the possibility of opening a new agency in Imperia, she was hesitant. The real estate market had been in serious crisis in recent years and she convinced her friend that it could be an imprudent decision. Opening a new office would also have diminished their quality of life, forcing them to work more for marginal profit.

Rachele frankly told her that it would be better to wait for better times to open a new office, dissuading her with these considerations. As a result, the project was abandoned, despite Marina's regret.

The years flew by, but her essence and self-love seemed to slow time's passage. She always found time for sports: she loved swimming and canoeing, which she practiced enthusiastically in the summer, and she almost always went to work by bicycle.

However, in addition to physical exercise, she was also mindful of her diet, preferring healthy, light foods. In this way, she kept her body slim and toned, appearing much younger than her age.

Her life seemed almost perfect: a job that suited her like a glove, newfound freedom, the esteem of many people and even her new, comfortable home.

And yet, Rachele felt there was still something missing in her existence. Her troubled relationship with Giorgio had left her wary and distant towards the opposite sex; perhaps this was one of the reasons for her lingering unease, which made her nights restless. She tried to ignore it, knowing that if she paid too much attention to it, she might question everything she had worked so hard to build.

Some men courted her, like Daniele, a kind and intelligent forty-eight-year-old dentist, recently single and without children. She had met him at a party at Paola's house, a mutual friend.

He had courted her in a gallant, but not oppressive way, and although Rachele felt a certain interest in him, she decided not to pursue the acquaintance further. Paola, who had introduced them, tried in vain to change her mind: «Rachele, you have to be able to open up… remember, not all men are like Giorgio», she had told her but Rachele didn't want to listen; she still wasn't ready to overcome her distrust.

However, without losing heart and without warning, one afternoon Daniele surprised her by showing up at her office. Like a true gentleman, he invited her for an aperitif by the sea. She was flattered and accepted, taking a break from work to enjoy the beautiful sunset in his company. They talked at length about their lives, interests and desires. Then, just before leaving the bar, Daniele invited her to the theatre the following Saturday. She looked at him hesitantly, so, to ease the tension, he added: «I'm just asking for a chance and if at the end of the evening you decide not to see me again, I promise I won't bother you anymore».

She looked at him intently for a long time, then, after a deep sigh, replied: «I'll think about it».

Over the following days, they spoke on the phone to confirm the date and, the next Saturday, Daniele picked her up to go to the theatre. They watched a comedy by a local troupe, *Il vero amico* by Carlo Goldoni, about the conflict between love and friendship.

At the end of the show, Rachele stood up, applauding ecstatically.

She often went to the theatre, loved the atmosphere and was fascinated by all kinds of performances.

They ended the evening at a bar, where they stopped for a drink. Seeing Rachele relaxed and smiling, Daniele felt confident that he had sparked her interest and, without hesitation, he leaned forward to kiss her.

Taken by surprise, she allowed him to kiss her for a moment, then, as the confusion passed, she quickly pulled away.

Aware of his mistake, Daniele hurried to apologise. «You're a lovely man and I had a wonderful time tonight, but I don't feel ready to go any further».

His expression showed deep disappointment and she, feeling a sense of guilt, explained that she still couldn't let go of her past and all that had hurt her. He tried to respond, but then decided to simply accompany her home, where they said goodbye awkwardly.

Then came the turn of Leonardo, the owner of a winery who went to the same gym as Rachele. He had also asked her out, but to avoid repeating what happened with Daniele, Rachele declined, agreeing only to a quick coffee after training.

Rachele retreated into herself, always giving the same explanation: «I'm not ready for a new relationship, I'm still too stressed from my past experience, I feel stuck, and I can't trust any man».

There was another factor that weighed heavily on Rachele's peace of mind: she didn't have a child, which, given her age, was at risk of remaining a mere dream. She felt a strong maternal instinct and had longed to be called "mum" for many years, but with a man like Giorgio, it had never been possible and now her coldness towards men left her feeling hopeless.

Another shadow over Rachele's life was her troubled relationship with her father, Gilberto, a stern and selfish man, stingy with both his emotions and money, a real disappointment as a parent. When she grew exasperated and took a job washing dishes at a restaurant to pay for her university studies, he didn't bat an eyelid.

He had almost never spoken kind words to her, offered encouragement, or given her compliments. On the contrary, he had always made her feel the burden of the money spent on her.

In the darkest moments of her relationship with Giorgio, Rachele often found herself reflecting on how those two men had negatively influenced her life.

Luckily, years had passed since the last time she had seen him, since her mother, Loriana, had literally sent him packing, demanding a divorce. Rachele had cut ties with him without the slightest remorse.

Loriana, who had retired a year earlier, moved to Sanremo to live near her older sister, now a widow. There, she met a sweet, caring man who looked after her in an almost touching way. In her heart, Rachele felt that her mother deserved this, after years of tribulations with her father, a man seldom by her side, leaving her to find the strength she needed.

This was unlike Rachele's experience a few years earlier when, after a breast ultrasound, she discovered a small lump.

Even then, she had not been able to count on anyone's support, especially not Giorgio, who had received the news with cold indifference.

The doctor overseeing her care had told her that she would probably need to undergo surgery. He prescribed further tests and recommended a course of treatment to follow for a few weeks.

Rachele hadn't mentioned anything to Marina either, partly because she wanted to wait for the test results and complete the treatment first. Moreover, being a very private and proud person, she didn't want to alarm anyone before having a definite answer.

Those were the longest days of her life. Endless sad thoughts wandered through her mind: it wasn't so much the fear of death, but of suffering, of enduring the treatments. She imagined that they might remove one of her breasts, even though cosmetic surgery could later help conceal the loss. Regardless, she was terrified that her life would never be the same again.

After those interminable weeks, she returned to the doctor, suitcase packed, ready to be admitted to the hospital. After ensuring that his patient had followed the prescribed treatment to the letter, the doctor performed a new ultrasound.

The visit was very thorough and the oncologist took his time before reaching a conclusion. As he examined the situation, Rachele noticed his expression change from incredulous to thoughtful.

Shortly after, with visible amazement, he delivered the verdict: «Miss... the lump has disappeared and the test results are negative».

He added that he had never seen anything like it and that, based on the results, Rachele was in excellent health. However, he recommended that she undergo periodic tests to keep things under control.

Rachele let herself go, hugging him and bursting into tears. She thanked him and left, feeling light and happy. She walked out of the doctor's office more serene and confident.

She wanted to run, carefree, and shout with joy, freeing herself from the anguish that had suffocated her, making her believe she was doomed.

Once home, she wanted to share the good news with Giorgio, but he was sitting on the sofa in front of the television, not even noticing her return.

With a newfound clarity, she decided not to share her joy with him, realising that he didn't deserve it.

Chapter Three

❖

Rachele believed that difficulties were opportunities for change, and her goal was to look to the future with confidence and optimism, feeling good about herself. She tried to shake off any negative feelings and the apathy that had plagued her for so long.

One of her greatest passions was travelling and, with no commitments other than work, she would occasionally book a getaway somewhere in the world.

One evening, after dinner, she was lying on the sofa watching TV. As she mechanically switched from one channel to another, she came across a documentary on the northeast of the Peloponnese, the largest Greek peninsula, known for its stunning nature, archaeological sites and coastlines. Those images captivated her so deeply that, without a second thought, she decided to book a vacation to that part of Greece, which she had yet to explore.

Not wanting to go alone, as she didn't like solitude, she thought of inviting two of her dearest friends on this adventure, who would almost certainly be thrilled to join her.

So, the following Saturday, she invited Pietro and Anna to dinner. Pietro was a forty-eight-year-old surveyor, separated, with a youthful appearance. He was tall and robust, not particularly handsome, but very charming. A fan of travel and archaeology, he also loved to have fun, especially at dance halls.

Anna, also forty-four and an architect, was dedicated to work and travel, with no romantic or family commitments. She had a very sweet disposition and was a polite, patient person.

During dinner, Rachele shared her idea, along with a detailed itinerary she had prepared.

The two friends exchanged a glance before accepting enthusiastically.

They discussed the trip at length to find two weeks that would work for all three of them, finally deciding to depart in early June.

Pietro and Anna gave Rachele complete freedom when it came to planning the trip. They had already travelled with her and knew they could trust her organisational skills. The weeks passed quickly. Marina, Rachele's partner, took about ten days off work for a trip to Spain with her new partner. There was a lot to do at the office, but the workload didn't weigh on her and, in the evenings after dinner, she always found time to plan the trip to Greece down to the smallest details.

She had the habit of packing her suitcase well in advance and, every evening, seeing it in her room, she meticulously added and selected the clothes and accessories she would take with her.

With only two days left until departure, she printed the plane tickets and accommodation bookings, took photos of everything, and divided the documents into two transparent, coloured folders.

When she left her office, she sent a message to Pietro and Anna: «Let's goooooo!». The two responded with equal enthusiasm: Pietro with a resounding «Come on!!» and Anna with «I can't wait!!!».

On 6 June, Rachele, Anna, and Pietro left Genoa airport on a flight to Athens.

They landed in the late morning, rented a car at the airport, a red, five-door Fiat Panda, and just over an hour later, they reached the first stop on their journey: the city of Corinth, where they would be staying for four days. They arrived at the hotel and went to their rooms. Rachele was enthusiastic, relaxed and eager to get moving right away and explore the place.

She unpacked her suitcase, then changed into a pair of soft jeans paired with a long, wide-sleeved burgundy shirt. She wore comfortable sneakers that matched her shirt.

She then left the room humming a tune and, after greeting the hotel staff in the lobby, headed out for a walk alone, as Pietro and Anna had decided to stay in their rooms to rest for a few hours, tired from the trip.

Along the way, she entered a shop resembling a Middle Eastern bazaar and, as she browsed, she found a book on the history of the Peloponnese in Italian. She bought it and, after paying, left the shop and continued walking with the book in hand.

She found a bench and decided to sit down to leaf through the book, discovering plenty of useful information for their vacation.

She stayed there for almost half an hour, then, feeling a bit tired, returned to the hotel.

That evening, they dined on the hotel terrace. The tables were elegantly set, with centrepieces featuring floating candles in hand-decorated glass vases. Additional candles had been placed along the entire low stone wall surrounding the terrace, along with some plants that added a romantic touch to the ambiance. They enjoyed a delicious grilled fish platter with baked potatoes, accompanied by a Greek white wine that perfectly complemented the fish.

In that moment, all three felt the vacation would be perfect: they were in a wonderful place where all they had to do was relax and have fun.

They chatted and joked while planning the excursions for the days ahead and went to bed just before midnight, agreeing to meet in the morning to explore the city of Corinth.

On the first few days, they dedicated themselves to excursions, starting, of course, with a visit to the city's archaeological area, one of the oldest and most important in Greece. In ancient times, Corinth had been a rich and powerful city that, thanks to its strategic location, had benefitted from great economic and cultural development.

They visited the Fountain of Pirene, a white marble monument linked to the legend of Pirene, a woman who, it is said, turned into a fountain because of the tears she shed for her son, Cenchriades, who was accidentally killed by Artemis.

Afterwards, they explored the Agora, then visited the Temple of Apollo, the archaeological museum and the Odeon. Lastly, they climbed to the top of the rocky hill where the fortress of Acrocorinth, the acropolis of ancient Corinth, stood, from which they admired the panorama of the Ionian and Aegean seas, the Strait of Corinth, the Isthmus, and the entire plain below.

The three friends looked around and realised they were completely alone; Pietro knew a cheerful Greek song and began to sing at the top of his voice.

Anna and Rachele accompanied him, dancing happily, experiencing the sweet sensation of being children again. They dedicated the third and fourth days to visiting the ruins of Mycenae, especially the mighty fortress governed by the Atreids, of which Agamemnon had been the most illustrious representative and leader of all the Greeks in the war against Troy. At the foot of the fortress, they visited some of the elaborate tombs of the kings and princes of Mycenae and, of course, the tomb of Agamemnon, called the Treasure of Atreus.

They stopped to admire the majestic Lion Gate, located along the Cyclopean walls, the entrance to the fortress of Mycenae and a symbol of the Mycenaean civilisation.

The three friends continued with a visit to the palace of the ruler of Mycenae, which was located right behind the Lion Gate.

Walking through those narrow passages, the stairways and entering the rooms of the royal palace, Rachele let her imagination run wild and she felt like she was reliving the splendour of the banquets at the court of Mycenae and hearing the footsteps of the fearsome warriors who had fought the war against Troy.

Pietro and Rachele walked slowly behind Anna, who was reading the story in the book purchased by her friend a few days earlier out loud.

Evening came and since they were starting to get hungry, they decided to skip the visit to the archaeological museum and return to their hotel, which was also in Corinth.

After a refreshing shower, they ate a hearty dinner on the terrace. Full and satisfied, they met in the reception lounge and decided the itinerary for the following day. The city of

Argos awaited them, where they would also stay the following night.

They left early and once they reached their destination, they immediately visited the cathedral of St Peter, located in the centre of the city; then, they walked towards the Ancient Theatre, which hosted political assemblies, but is known throughout the world as the site of the Nemean Games, during which sports, singing and poetry competitions were held.

Struck by the steep steps leading up the hill of Larissa, they walked up to the highest point of the theatre to enjoy the splendid view of the city.

Between videos and photos, they remained there for almost an hour. Later, they visited the castle of Argos, nestled on the top of the hill of Larissa. Lastly, at Anna's insistence, they visited the archaeological museum which housed wonderful artefacts from the Mycenaean and classical civilisations.

In the afternoon, they made a long stop in the ancient city of Tiryns, located southeast of Argos. A visit to the site of the city was a must for them, as they were lovers of archaeology. Consulting the tourist guide, they were fascinated by the legend regarding the city, which says it was founded by Proteus, the brother of Acrisius, king of Argos. Tiryns, which was at its zenith in the Mycenaean era, was often subjugated by Argos and was destroyed in the first half of the fifth century BC, then abandoned. Anna and Rachele's gaze was immediately captured by the imposing, evocative cyclopean wall, over seven metres high and extraordinarily well preserved, which they walked along on some of the sections that were still accessible.

Having absorbed so much history and culture, on the sixth day they continued their journey and dedicated themselves to leisure and the sea. They travelled along the road that led to Tripoli, a mountainous and very scenic route, from where they admired the magnificent view that merges into the Aegean Sea.

Towards mid-afternoon, they arrived at the beautiful tourist resort of Kalamata, located in the Messenia region and overlooking the Ionian Sea, renowned for its beaches and nightlife. The clear waters, the imposing presence of the nearby mountains and the alternating large beaches and semi-hidden rocky coves made it even more beautiful. It conveyed an emotion that felt like freedom.

Chapter Four

They arrived at the hotel where they would stay for a week. Their rooms overlooked the indoor swimming pool and the three friends really appreciated the view. Rachele finally felt flooded with the desire to live life that she had always had, but that had faded in recent years. Perhaps she was once more becoming the determined woman she used to be, the one who was always up for anything, eager to meet people and experience every emotion to the fullest.

She smiled as she looked at herself in the mirror, amazed and incredulous because a few days earlier she wouldn't have believed it possible to find so much enthusiasm and well-being in such a short time.

Since it was already evening, they decided to have dinner at an outdoor restaurant with live music: it was very cosy, crowded with people and, as they would later discover, the food was very good.

At the entrance, a large poster promoted a dance evening in the outdoor room of the place, where an Anglo-Saxon group playing '80s English pop music would perform.

As was customary since their arrival in Greece, they ate a fish-based dinner and, once the meal was over, decided to stay and spend the rest of the evening there.

They sat on high stools at the bar facing the dance floor and ordered something to drink.

Intoxicated by the music, Rachele was dancing on her chair, happily enjoying herself, when a man sat down next to her.

Not realising he was there, she accidentally elbowed him.

She turned around quickly, ready to apologise, but the words disappeared. The stranger, with a serious, austere, but tremendously charming look, smiled at her with infinite sweetness, murmuring something in English. She stared at him for a few moments, discovering with some embarrassment that she was blushing. She mumbled something and immediately looked forward again.

The man seemed to appreciate her liveliness and, every time Rachele turned shyly towards him, she noticed that his curious gaze was almost always directed at her.

Her heart in turmoil, she told herself that, despite the somewhat restrained expression on his face, he was extremely attractive.

Ultimately, he was the one to break the ice. Extending his hand, he introduced himself and stated his name:

"Ryan".

Rachele looked at him with a shy smile and she also said her name.

He added something and, with dismay, Rachele realised that, not knowing the English language, it was almost impossible to communicate.

The man understood and, to remedy the situation, took her hand and led her to the centre of the dance floor, where they let themselves be captivated by the music.

They danced for a long time, under the incredulous eyes of Pietro and Anna, enjoying themselves like a couple of youngsters.

After a good half hour, they went back to sit on the stools. Anna and Pietro also joined them. Rachele introduced them, and with the help of her friend, who spoke excellent English, they were able to start communicating. The man ordered a bottle of Retsina, an excellent Greek wine, from the waiter, they exchanged brief information to get to know each other better, then at around two they all left the premises, took a short walk together by the sea, accompanied by the glow of the lights reflecting on the water. Ryan exchanged a few more words in English with Pietro and asked him if they could meet again the next evening at the same place because he had enjoyed their company and he would also have been very happy to see Rachele again.

Pietro translated the man's wish to his friend and she nodded, accepting with pleasure. Finally, with a satisfied smile, Ryan said goodbye and left.

Rachele couldn't sleep that night: her thoughts kept returning to the picture of that charming man's face, that warm smile that had confused her. She had learned that he was Irish, from Dublin to be precise, that he was fifty- one years old and owned a company, without going into further detail. She fell asleep when the sun had already begun to lighten the sky.

The next morning, the only goal the three friends had was to lie down on the beach, enjoying the sun and the sea, so they decided to rent beach umbrellas and sun loungers. Since the sea was calm, in the late morning they decided to go for a ride in a canoe.

They rented three canoes of different colours: Pietro's was blue, Rachele's was yellow and Anna's was so red that they looked like an absurd Romanian flag floating on the sea. After an hour of paddling, they returned exhausted but happy and went to lie down under their beach umbrellas, falling onto the sun loungers like dead weights.

«I'm far too old for this sort of thing!», Pietro declared, closing his eyes. «Don't be silly!», Rachele retorted. «You're still a youngster. In fact... we're all youngsters! I bet we could do it again this afternoon!». «Don't count on me», Anna replied. «If I try that again, I'll have a heart attack!». Pietro and Rachele laughed. «Don't be so dramatic!». After a well-deserved rest, they went to a small spot near the beach where they enjoyed hearty Greek salads. Although they had pretended nothing had happened all morning, Anna and Pietro could no longer resist the temptation to joke about the handsome man Rachele had met the night before: «Come on, Rachele, what do you think of this Ryan guy? He certainly made an impression on you, didn't he?».

She pretended to be annoyed, but the smug smile that crept across her face didn't go unnoticed for long. «You're also very happy to see him again, right?», Pietro said slyly. Rachele nodded. «Good for you!», Anna said happily to her friend. «He really is quite a handsome man, and he seems interesting… though we definitely need to find out more about him!».

«Yes, that's true... but I don't speak English!», Rachele replied in a resigned tone. «I'll take care of that!», Pietro reassured her, as he was fluent in English. «Just don't make me look bad!», she said with a smile, grateful for her friends' support.

English had never been a problem for her until that moment. No matter where she went in the world, she always managed to make herself understood in one way or another. However, it had almost always involved asking for directions or occasionally going into a shop to buy something. In any case, she had always travelled with people who spoke the language. Therefore, she had never had to worry about it. She realised that it was the first time she had met a man outside her own country and that, perhaps, that language she had never learned would really have come in handy this time.

By evening, the three friends had already arrived early at the meeting place. As soon as they entered, Rachele began to look around anxiously and when she saw him, he was already walking towards her, slowly, looking at her with a satisfied expression; the emotion and joy of seeing him again increased beyond measure.

He greeted her with an affectionate gesture, similar to a hug, showing off his charming smile.

During the evening, they tried to get to know each other better once again and, thanks to Pietro's help, Rachele learned that he was the manager of a real estate company in Dublin and that he was there for work. With the help of her friend once again, Rachele informed him that she lived in Savona, owned a company, and was there on holiday, but didn't want to disclose further details about her life.

They let themselves be carried away by the music and danced for a long time that evening, to the point that Anna and Pietro, despite being engrossed in dancing themselves, almost felt like they were in the way. Feeling tired and hot, Pietro suggested that the group sit at one of the tables outside the bar to have a drink together.

From the attentions that Ryan paid to Rachele, it was perfectly clear that he wanted to enjoy her company as long as possible, but due to the difficulty in communicating, he relied on Pietro's help.

Ryan tried in vain to ask for her phone number, but given the woman's unwillingness, he didn't insist. Even though she felt a strong attraction, scruples, common sense, and fears of various kinds led her to stall. As he spoke to Pietro, Ryan confided that he was very attracted to Rachele; he found her both beautiful and intriguing. Anna listened to this admission and discreetly leaned closer to her friend to share what Ryan had said; flattered, she smiled and gazed at the man, trying not to lend too much importance to the matter, but she was very torn: on the one hand, she wanted to find out as much as possible about him, while on the other, she wanted either to run away or to treat him with indifference, because the emotion she felt looking into his eyes made her afraid of losing control. At the end of the evening, they stood up and left the table; once again, they said goodbye, making a date for the next day, but before leaving, Ryan gave her a kiss on the cheek and unexpectedly held her in a gentle embrace. He then turned to thank Pietro for his help, and Pietro, for his part, began to enjoy the company of the Irishman, who for some reason felt trustworthy, and despite barely knowing him, he sensed that perhaps he could be the right man for Rachele. As they walked back to the residence, with Pietro arm in arm with the two women, Rachele admitted: 'You know, I really like him... even though I can't speak to him directly. But honestly, I think it's all complete madness!». «Rachele, it's not madness!», Pietro replied seriously, «it's just life! Enjoy these wonderful emotions without overthinking things!».

Chapter Five

The next day, laziness took over, and for the entire morning, their only refuge was the sun loungers and beach umbrellas. Around midday, they decided to take a short swim and, an hour later, they headed to the usual place on the beach to eat that Greek salad they loved so much. Rachele went back to retrieve the hat she had left on the sun lounger. While walking quickly and distractedly back to the bar, she bumped into a man. She was wearing large sunglasses and a hat, making her hard to recognise, but Ryan spotted her almost immediately and stopped her with an outstretched arm.

«Rachele?».

She looked at him in surprise and almost wanted to hug him, but she controlled herself. «Ryan!», she replied, smiling happily.

Then he began speaking in English, and she lowered her eyes in discouragement. He pointed towards the bar where Anna and Pietro were waiting for her. Following her, and realising he hadn't eaten yet, he decided to take advantage of the situation and join them.

«Finally, a meeting during the day,' Rachele thought to herself, «I can observe him a little better.».

The man seemed very pleased with that fortuitous meeting; the four of them ordered a large Greek salad, joking about the remarks Pietro and Ryan made in English, which Anna translated into Italian with some effort for Rachele.

They then also ordered some excellent ice cream and Greek coffee for everyone. Ryan held Rachele's hand tightly for a moment, looking into her eyes intensely, trying to convey a message. Even though she was embarrassed, she didn't move her hand away, thereby giving him a sign of approval. Shortly after, they got up to return to their spot on the beach. Ryan accompanied them to spend a few more minutes in the woman's company, then said goodbye, as he had commitments at work.

The three friends went back to rest on the sun loungers, sheltered by two large beach umbrellas.

After a relaxing afternoon, they made their way back to their accommodation, stopping at a quaint bar on the beach for a quick aperitif. Then, they went back to freshen up and plan the evening.

They decided to have dinner at a small, quaint restaurant near their residence. During dinner, Anna and Pietro teased Rachele, provoking her with ironic jokes about Ryan.

«You know that he's even more handsome in the light of day?», Anna said.

«What do you think, friend? You're too silent and pensive!», Pietro added, «I can see from a mile away that you're confused, dazed ...», he continued.

At that point, Rachele loosened up, openly freeing her thoughts: «Okay! I can confirm that I like him a lot and it's making me a bit agitated, that's all! Now, stop giving me grief, I need to understand what's happening to me a little better».

After dinner, they went to the place where they were meeting Ryan for the third time.

They took a seat near the bar, and a bit later, he arrived as well. Rachele spotted him from a distance, giving her time to take in his appearance: he was dressed in dark blue cotton trousers and a light jacket of the same color, with a white shirt underneath. He walked slowly, wearing his usual captivating smile. When she saw him, a shiver of happiness ran through Rachele's body.

All four sat in the same seats, as if they had been reserved exclusively for them. They listened to the music, slowly sipping their cocktails or their beer.

Their gazes seemed intense and complicit and Rachele hoped that Ryan also shared the same joy that she was feeling.

The band that evening had a wide and varied repertoire of songs. The most popular were English and American songs, and Ryan often joined in with the chorus.

At a certain point, he approached the band and spoke to the singer. The latter nodded and a few moments later performed a song by Gary Moore called "Still Got The Blues".

Ryan asked her to dance and, in the centre of the dance floor, emotion overwhelmed them and they gazed into each others' eyes almost magically. Then he began to sing, and the sweetness of his voice dissolved any hesitation Rachele felt; it was a sweet, romantic moment and everything seemed perfect: she prayed that the magic would never end. The passionate attitude that shone through in the man enveloped Rachele and her rational caution began to falter.

Back at the table, Anna and Pietro were happy to admire the passion that was developing between the two. Rachele experienced a powerful mix of contrasting emotions—fear and joy.

Fear, because Ryan was nevertheless a stranger; joy, because his closeness caused continuous jolts to her heart, sensations that she found she no longer wanted to escape. As they danced in the crowd, their minds were confused and wandered in search of a lost sense of balance. Their long, profound gazes, their knowing smiles, their hands that sought each other with fervent desire.

Nothing felt mundane or predictable, as both were fully immersed in every moment of that dance, full of glances and caresses, with the intensity of a fire capable of warming even the coldest hearts.

It had become late, they knew that the time had come to end the evening, yet they found it difficult to part. Taking her hand, the man walked with her, joining Anna and Pietro. He accompanied them to the door of their accommodation, then he drew close to her gently in the darkness and silence of the night, he brushed her lips with a tender kiss and their knowing glances spoke for them. The next morning, Anna suggested they go to the city on a shopping trip. Pietro was enthusiastic about the idea, while Rachele preferred to stay on the beach, where she spent the whole morning, fantasizing about Ryan, wondering where he was and what he was doing. At times she would lift her head and look at the people around her, hoping to see him.

«Just like a young girl...», she murmured to herself, confused.

At a certain point, someone behind her covered her eyes with his hands: she wasn't surprised and immediately understood who it was. He politely sat down on her lounger and said: «Beautiful woman, how are you?», then, seeing that she was alone, he pulled her into his arms and kissed her tenderly. She couldn't help herself and surrendered. They stayed there, lying on the same bed, for almost an hour, holding each other in their arms and looking at each other in silence, with him stroking her hair softly.

When he left, Rachele took a walk along the shoreline. Anna and Pietro returned for lunch, joined their friend at the usual bar for a snack, then spent the afternoon on the beach.

They climbed onto the rocks and had a diving competition. They quickly climbed up a steel ladder placed between the rocks and dived repeatedly, laughing and carefree. Rachele and Anna didn't hesitate to jump into the water, while

Pietro was a little more hesitant, prompting the two to tease him: «Come on, how long do you need to wait before jumping in every time?? You're as slow as a snail!!!», «You're not turning into a scaredy- cat, are you??».

«Scaredy-cat, me?? Of course not!! It's just that I don't want to make you look bad!», he replied every time with a smile on his lips.

«Yeah, right!», Anna said. Then, taking him completely by surprise, she pushed him, making him fall into the water. Rachele burst out laughing... so, Anna pushed her, too, before also diving in. They played in the water, playing pranks on each other, having fun like a bunch of adolescents.

Pietro then teased Rachele: «I wonder if Ryan knows how to swim! Aren't you curious to see him in a swimsuit?» Not to be outdone, Anna joined in: «In my opinion, even though we've only ever seen him dressed... he has a great body! One of those men who certainly doesn't go unnoticed!»

Rachele replied smugly: «Since I can't ask him anything, you ask him a few questions about swimming... otherwise what kind of friends are you!», adding ironically, «As for his body, well... I've already seen him bare-chested and he didn't disappoint!».

«Whaaat?», «When???», the two friends shouted together, «Where did you see him? What did you do? You naughty little thing... you don't tell us anything... what a friend you are!!».

They almost drowned her jokingly.

«Now we're getting out of the water to question you, you can't escape!», Anna said with the curiosity of a child.

They got out and lay down on their sun loungers with an air of satisfaction, the two friends eager for the latest update.

«Ryan was passing by, undoubtedly not by chance, saw that I was alone and stayed with me for an hour. We kissed and embraced on the sun lounger in silence. We weren't able to talk, anyway... We couldn't understand each other!! That's all, I swear».

«Oh, right! You didn't waste any time, then!», said Pietro.

«Yesss, I was sure it would happen! I'm so happy!!», Anna exclaimed.

While they were talking about what had happened, the sun slowly set, so they returned to their accommodation and carefully got ready for the evening. Rachele chose her clothing with great attention, because she wanted to be elegant and accentuate her charm.

She decided to wear a black dress with a neckline that was tastefully modest, three-quarter sleeves, slightly fitted, and falling to her calves. To add a touch of colour, she chose a beautiful necklace with large pink pearls and matching earrings. Lastly, she put on a steel watch with a pink face.

She wore a pair of black décolleté shoes, high and open-toed, which highlighted her pink-painted toenails. Lastly, she chose a small black handbag.

She left her room and met her friends, who were also elegant and refined, at the entrance of the residence.

They were very complimentary towards her and Pietro bent down and kissed her hand, like a true gentleman, and mischievously exclaimed: «Ryan doesn't stand a chance tonight!».

Pietro, who was proud of the elegance and beauty of his friends, took them both by the arm and headed out, ready to experience a new, exciting evening.

By mutual agreement, they decided to have dinner in a restaurant that had been recommended by an Italian who was on holiday like them and who they had met on the beach of the residence. The place was sophisticated, with food that was strictly fish-based, generous and tasty.

After dinner, they got up from the table to take a short walk along the seafront and then headed to the usual, by now familiar bar.

Seeing Rachele arrive in all her splendor, Ryan moved towards her eagerly and, unexpectedly, embraced her passionately.

Thanks to Pietro and Anna's mediation, during the evening they discovered that, as well as being an excellent swimmer, he was also a fan of scuba diving. He also confided in Pietro, admitting that he was very interested in Rachele, that he thought she was a bright and extremely attractive woman, adding that he liked her smile, how she moved, and that being in her company made him feel alive and gave him unexpected emotions. Ryan asked Pietro to tell his friend about these strong feelings to see if she also felt the same. Rachele felt flattered and blushed; she had never spoken to a man through someone who translated their thoughts and emotions, and she was unable to give a composed reply. So, she simply restricted herself to a shy nod, and, although she hadn't said a single word, her radiant gaze spoke more than words ever could.

Sporting a satisfied expression, Ryan affectionately put an arm around her shoulders and led her to the dance floor.

They danced carefree, embracing each other without a thought for anyone around them who might be looking at them with interest and curiosity. The beautiful music surrounding them heightened the intensity to the point where the two seemed almost in love.

Rachele's desire was growing, though she felt a deep anger at being unable to speak to him as she would have liked. Her curiosity and the need to ask him so many questions, to know everything about him, about his life, and also to share something about herself, were too strong. His discomfort was also evident, as he whispered words to her and then looked up at the sky, sighing with resignation and disappointment, because they couldn't understand each other!

So, he limited himself to singing the most beautiful songs that accompanied their dancing, trying to convey to her the emotions he felt.

At a certain point, they embraced each other tightly and he seized the moment to give her a passionate kiss on the lips; his desire had become all too clear.

Rachele realised that she wanted to let go, and surrender herself completely, dispel any scruple, any fear, any prejudice, any sense of modesty, and let herself be loved... but the sweet, romantic music stopped and, for no apparent reason, dissolved the enchantment of that moment.

Without saying a word, Ryan took her hand and they went outside together, in silence, walking until they reached a parapet overlooking the sea. They caressed each other's hands, intertwining their fingers, lulled by the sweet melody of the waves crashing on the rocks, and kissed passionately. However, the magical moment was interrupted by the arrival of Pietro and Anna; they pulled away from each other, embarrassed, they pulled away from each other, and everyone decided to head to the hotel. Naturally, Ryan accompanied them, holding Rachele's hand... The two friends went inside first, leaving them alone again. The two embraced once more in the dark, in a silence broken only by their sighs and their profound, infinite kisses. Then, they were forced to part, and Rachele entered her hotel.

Chapter Six

The three friends dedicated the last day of their vacation to the seaside and total relaxation. As they went to the beach, they were overcome by a sense of melancholy: the following day, they would have to return home to their everyday lives.

They joked around, but the enjoyment of that day was not as carefree as the previous ones. Especially for Rachele, that day felt like an alarm clock reminding her that she had to get up, that everything was coming to an end, and she would soon return to reality. She felt pensive and confused; she felt like a teenager who had found her first love on vacation and didn't want to let him go. Yet, she knew that it wasn't just that. She hadn't experienced those feelings for a long time. Could it be that it was just a fleeting summer romance? Tormented and distracted by those thoughts, she was unable to fully enjoy that last day, which flew by quickly.

After having dinner in one of the restaurants on the seafront, they went to the usual bar to spend their last evening and meet their Irish friend for the final time. Pietro and Anna had grown quite fond of him, and for Pietro, it was also a way to practice his English with someone; she, on the other hand, was happy to observe the magical attraction that was blossoming between her friend and that handsome man.

They entered the bar and saw him sitting at a table with two men. Rachele scrutinised them: from their features they must have been Greek.

Ryan immediately noticed Rachele's presence and, after saying something to the other two, he got up to go to her. He kissed her softly on the cheek, then, through Pietro, he let them know that he was there with two of his customers.

«I'll be with you shortly», he said.

Rachele watched him walk away, feeling a pang of disappointment. It would be their last evening together and she didn't think it was right for him to waste time with anyone other than her.

«Come on Rachele, let's go get a drink», Anna said, taking her arm. «He'll be here soon enough», she added, sensing her friend's disappointment.

They sat down at the counter and ordered a beer. Rachele tried to enjoy the carefree atmosphere in the bar, but Ryan's absence had upset her and, with a little too much impatience, she kept glancing towards his table, hoping that he would get rid of those people as soon as possible.

Finally, after what seemed like an eternity, he said goodbye to his two customers, then took a chair and joined Rachele and the others. He called on a waiter and ordered a bottle of excellent sparkling wine to toast the beautiful evenings they had spent together. He knew this would be the last, since his Italian friends would be leaving the next morning. He raised his glass and Pietro translated his short speech: «I'm happy to have met you. You've been lovely to me and great company these evenings. I'm especially happy to have met Rachele, who has aroused an emotion in me that I've never felt».

Listening to those words, Rachele felt her heart swell with joy, and at that very moment, she sensed a new chapter beginning in her life.

That evening, neither of them wanted to part from the other: they danced, joked as much as the language barrier would allow, but never spent a single moment apart.

Magically, Gary Moore's song Still Got the Blues began to play. The two of them, as if it were completely natural, held each other in their arms, isolating themselves from the rest of the world, engulfed only in their shared passion.

She was tender, he was passionate, both shaken by overwhelming emotions, aware that this was their last night together. Rachele, overcome by an intense shiver that she couldn't remember ever having felt before, which ran through her entire body, decided she wouldn't hold back; she would savor every moment of that magical night.

Ryan also seemed to feel the same sensations, his eyes expressed joy, his smile was bright and, with slight apprehension, he whispered a few words to her, thinking she would interpret them correctly.

Rachele understood, looked at him almost hypnotised, and answered:

«Yes».

Without waiting any longer, he took her hand and together they left the bar, far from the din of the music and the people.

They were alone, hand in hand, walking without stopping, and Rachele felt as if she were watching the most romantic of films, in which she was the protagonist. However, completely unexpected and unwanted, her old fear returned, a fear that for so long had prevented her from fully grasping the opportunities that came her way. She felt a mix of happiness and fear, a profound internal conflict that was capable of calling into question everything that was happening.

She felt a mix of happiness and fear—a profound internal conflict capable of questioning everything that was happening.

She sighed as she continued to follow him and she began to walk more slowly, her breathing laboured. She prayed that he was the man she hoped he was and that he wouldn't hurt her.

They were alone, her friends were no longer there to protect her... she was at the mercy of this man who kept moving forwards, almost as if he were running from something unknown, taking her with him.

She half-closed her eyes, her heart was beating like crazy, she turned her head, hoping to see Pietro and Anna behind her.

They weren't there, of course.

She stared at Ryan's back and thought back to the kisses they had shared earlier, the emotion she had felt when their lips met, how he tasted, the way he had looked at her, the joy she had seen in his eyes.

Then, she suddenly stopped, letting go of his hand, which she had held tightly all evening.

He turned around with a surprised look and met her gaze, perceiving all the fears she was experiencing.

He took her hand again, placed it on his heart and shook his head.

It was then that she understood: he would never hurt her and despite the doubts that had tried to surface, she was ready to follow him without any hesitation.

She was ready for anything that might happen.

They reached a busy street and Ryan hailed a taxi with a gesture of his hand.

They got in: he sat Rachele in the back seat, while he sat in front, not letting go of her hand for a single moment, as if to reassure her.

In a few minutes, they arrived at an elegant residence.

Ryan paid the fare, then helped her out of the car. Still in silence, they went inside, heading towards what could only be his accommodation.

The first thing that caught Rachele's eye was the spectacular view from the terrace, and the enchantment of the night panorama sent another powerful shiver through her entire body.

The apartment was delightful, elegant, and cosy, and she was with a man whom she thought was wonderful. A man whom, she knew, she desired with every fibre of her being—there was no use lying to herself.

They looked at each other intensely, their gazes speaking a universal language—the language of passion. In those long minutes of a magical atmosphere, Rachele realised the importance of silence, the teacher of truth.

Silence.

Panting, hearts beating as one.

Silence.

Their lips searched each other out, finding each other intensely. Passion grew like the desire to become a single essence.

Their souls resonated with the same vibrations, filling them both with the sweetest and most profound emotions.

«I love you», Ryan whispered, caressing her hair.

«Ti amo», Rachele replied in Italian.

They stared at each other for a moment longer, then all trace of fear vanished, and they made love with inexhaustible passion, knowing they belonged to each other.

Chapter Seven

The thought of getting up and leaving that reassuring, protective, passionate embrace, the thought of walking away from Ryan's intense, penetrating gaze, the thought that in a few hours she would be leaving, were like the sharp bite of an animal on living prey. The only way to escape that torment was to leave the room as quickly as possible. So, she jumped up, grabbed her clothes, and hurriedly dressed.

Surprised by her behaviour, he got out of the bed. He began to pace back and forth across the room, muttering incomprehensible phrases.

She stopped for a moment, looked at him sadly and, with eyes swollen with tears, took a piece of paper from her bag and wrote down her phone number.

She left it on the bed and he nodded, as if to say that he would call her. That they would hear from each other, that they wouldn't lose sight of each other.

They kissed for the last time, then Rachele, without turning around, ran away: she was sure that if she had looked into his wonderful eyes one more time, she would never have left.

A few minutes later, she was on the street, walking briskly, her mind numb with tiredness and the weight of separation. Having walked a sufficient distance, she stopped, caught her breath, and, looking back, gazed at the residence where she had spent that unique, extraordinary night. She looked at the balcony where, just a few hours earlier, she had been held tightly in his arms, admiring the romantic night-time landscape, with lights reflecting on the seafront. A dark despair overcame her, leaving her exhausted.

She regretted leaving him so hastily; she regretted not making love to him one last time. She regretted not having stayed in his arms, not having waited a little longer to try to make him understand that she would never forget him and that, in fact, she was ready to wait for him just to be with him again.

A tear ran down her cheek. Determined, she started walking again, without turning around. He would call; he would look for her—she was sure of it…

She got back to her room, took a shower and packed her suitcase without thinking; after a little over an hour she was ready to leave.

She drummed up some courage and continued her journey in silence. She got into a taxi with her friends to go to the airport in Kalamata.

Pietro and Anna gave her curious looks, but they avoided asking any questions: it was clear to both of them how deeply upset she was.

During the trip, in the long hours of reflection, she began to metabolise her experience.

She withdrew into herself, allowing her thoughts to wander.

She would have liked to tell him that just one night had been enough to reawaken feelings that she no longer believed she still had.

Then, she thought to herself: *"Did you have to come from another country to open my heart? And now that you've done so? Was it all in vain? A night of passion during a vacation?*

And yet, our eyes, our smiles, our hands, our lips were enough to speak for us, it was more than just one night, it couldn't be otherwise. Something so beautiful certainly can't end today, in this way!".

As much as she tried to convince herself that it had been a wonderful experience, she burst into tears.

Seated by the window on the plane, she managed to hide her face, careful not to draw attention. Her friends, sitting next to her, witnessed the outburst and tried to comfort her.

«You should be happy that you experienced such strong emotions! You'll hear from each other very soon, you'll see, and I'm sure you'll meet again!», Anna whispered, squeezing her hand.

Pietro also reassured her, saying that it was clear as day that Ryan wouldn't disappear from her life.

Grateful for the comfort of her friends, she got up to take shelter and compose herself in the plane's bathroom for a few minutes. As she closed herself in the small room, she thought that Pietro and Anna were right: they would meet again; it couldn't be otherwise.

Fate couldn't be so cruel as to have made her meet a wonderful man only to then lose him forever.

They landed at Genoa airport in the early afternoon and, after collecting their bags, had a coffee at the bar. During the journey that would take them back to Savona, they talked about the vacation and how much fun they had, carefully avoiding any mention of Ryan.

Once in the city, Pietro accompanied Rachele home. They hugged goodbye, and then she entered her building. Once inside, she dropped her suitcase at the entrance and, remembering that there was practically nothing edible in the house, decided to go to the nearby supermarket.

She bought the bare essentials for dinner and quickly returned to her apartment, without even saying a word to any of the neighbours she met along the way, something quite unusual for her.

She unpacked her suitcase, feeling a sharp sense of nostalgia every time she touched the clothes she had worn during the evenings spent with him. She would have given anything to go back and relive every moment of that experience.

She thought back to the evening they had met, when she had accidentally bumped into him. She wished she could hear him sing again, especially Gary Moore's song. It was a wish she feared would never come true, as he could easily have decided not to reach out again.

«Don't be silly!», she admonished herself, forcing herself not to cry. «If fate wants it, you'll meet again; otherwise, it will remain a beautiful memory!». In order not to go crazy, she decided it was better to avoid daydreaming about the future and concentrate on the present and on the things she had to do.

She prepared something to eat, took a shower and slipped into her bed as if it were a safe haven, but she had a terrible night. She couldn't sleep; she could still feel his breathing, his scent and every sensation she had felt the night before.

Memories overwhelmed her; his absence was a relentless pain, fears tormented her.

Her mind was prey to a thousand thoughts that not only prevented her from falling asleep, but also from breathing, as if the weight of that absence was strangling her.

Too many emotions in such a short space of time. She had moved from fear to happiness, then to detachment, and finally a great sense of desperation.

She got up more than once, cursing herself for not being able to accept being far apart; tears accompanied her discomfort and she welcomed the rising sun as a true blessing.

When dawn began to paint the sky, she went down to walk along the seafront, absorbed in memories that were still vivid; looking intensely at the rough sea that violently crashed against the rocks only fueled her dark moment of desperation. She fought hard against the suffering that was nesting inside her, to the point that it caused her physical discomfort…

Chapter Eight

❖

Her days began to pass quickly, without purpose; little by little, she became aware of the change that was happening to her: that encounter had transformed her, she found it difficult to concentrate, she forgot things, she felt a constant anxiety that didn't give her a moment's peace. Surprised by the intensity of that feeling, she couldn't understand how it was possible to experience such passion for a someone she had only just met, —a feeling made even more frustrating by the fact that Ryan hadn't gotten in touch and, in a moment of despair, she even thought that, in her haste to get away that morning, she might have written down her phone number incorrectly. Her confusion increased with all those doubts and lapses of memory. To ease the sense of impotence that was torturing her, she began doing some online research: she wanted to find information on all the real estate companies in Dublin. If luck were on her side, she would be able to find out which one was Ryan's and try to track him down. She discovered that there was a surprising number of real estate companies in the Irish city; however, without losing heart, she carried out a thorough investigation, studying them one by one.

The result was inconclusive; she didn't find any useful information and thought to herself that perhaps Ryan merely worked at one, without being the owner.

She carefully considered what her next move could be, even if, all told, she couldn't come up with an answer, except that she missed that man terribly and that perhaps he had just wanted to have a little fun.

The weeks passed by quickly and monotonously, with Rachele trying to make peace with herself and turn the page, because it was now clear that it had been nothing more than a simple one-night stand for him and everything he had made her believe had the sole purpose of getting her into bed.

However, it was a thought that didn't convince her, because she knew what she had seen in his eyes and what she had felt in those intense, endless embraces. She couldn't accept that fate had been so mocking.

No. Impossible, and she told herself that, somehow, in the end everything would be resolved... she just needed to hold on and have faith.

Feeling reassured by those thoughts, she tried to pick herself up and give a new meaning to her life: she began to dedicate herself entirely to work, putting in the utmost effort, taking part in every event that, in one way or another, was linked to her business.

She attended inaugurations, lunches and dinners with colleagues; moreover, she had organised some meetings herself long ago. with experts in the real estate and financial sectors, men and women who could somehow contribute to the recovery of a sector, the real estate sector, which was still suffering from the restrictions of the economic crisis in recent years.

On weekends her mind was focused solely on sporting activities: gym, swimming pool and bike rides. She filled her days to distract herself from other thoughts, but at night, when she was alone in her apartment, lying in a bed that was too big and empty, the face of her sweet Irishman never left her, causing immense restlessness that tore at her soul.

One morning, while she was looking at the photos she had taken during the holiday, she had a stroke of genius: From what she had gathered and remembered, Ryan was in Greece on business; therefore, she decided to focus her search on Dublin real estate companies that operated internationally, not just in Ireland.

Incredibly, that new approach led her to a single, interesting result: *Irish International Business*, a multinational company that operated in several sectors, including real estate. It was a gigantic company, which operated in all the countries in the European Union and the United States. Not surprisingly, the site was available in all European languages.

After selecting Italian and clicking on the Irish International real estate staff, she discovered a certain Ryan Walsh, co-manager for the Mediterranean area.

Bingo! Maybe she had hit the nail on the head! She double-checked more carefully, hoping to find at least one photo of him, but all she got was an e-mail address:

ryanwalsh@iib.com.

Her heart pounding and her breathing labored, she felt she was on the right track and that perhaps that might be her Ryan's e-mail address, so she immediately decided to send him a message. She didn't know English, but, for what she intended to write, Google Translate would more than suffice.

She asked him if he was the same Ryan she had met in Greece. She wrote down her phone number once more, then said goodbye, adding that she hoped to hear from him soon. Her heart fluttered as she pressed the send button: a new wait began, perhaps more agonizing than the last. Yet, she realised she felt calmer now. There was a new spark of hope.

Unfortunately, the days passed, but there was no response.

Disappointed and heartbroken, she tried once again to accept it and move forward, doing her best to think about him as little as possible.

To distract herself, she decided to organise a pleasant evening with Marina, Pietro, and Anna, who brought along a friend, Sauro, whom she had planned to meet that very evening.

«Do you mind if he comes, too?», Anna asked.

«No, of course not! Besides, the more the merrier!», she said; she knew Sauro by sight and from what she remembered, he was a rather nice man. «Thanks Rachele, you're a sweetheart».

They said goodbye and agreed to meet at nine o'clock that evening.

Rachele had thought about preparing dinner herself, but an unexpected work call kept her busy for most of the afternoon, so she sent a message to her and they all agreed to opt for the best pizzeria in Savona.

They spent a lovely evening, laughing and joking, especially thanks to Sauro, who was unsurpassed when it came to telling jokes. What slightly disturbed Rachele was the fact that some of that man's expressions at times reminded her of Ryan and, although she tried to hide it, a veil of sadness darkened her face.

«Is there something wrong?», Anna whispered in her ear. «No…. everything's fine», she lied, but her friend's gaze betrayed that she didn't believe her. So, she confided that he had never got back in touch, told her about the e-mail she had sent to someone called Ryan Walsh, whom she had found online, and also mentioned the ongoing silence. Her friend looked at her for a long time, but she sensed it wasn't the right moment to discuss such a delicate matter. «After dinner, I'll stop by your place, and we'll chat for a bit, alright?» She nodded gratefully.

At the end of the evening, the two women were sat on Rachele's couch.

«I think I was just a one-night stand», she said after a long silence. «Otherwise, why wouldn't he call?».

Anna sighed, then searched for the right words to avoid hurting her even more: «Yes, probably... but you can't say for sure! If he really works for that multinational, he'll have very little free time, and he might even be on the other side of the world, closing deals you can't even imagine! I know it's difficult because you're in love, but maybe you just need to be patient and wait».

She took her hand, squeezing it gently. «If it's fate, you'll meet each other again...» and then the hardest part, «otherwise you'll have to find the strength to move on and view Ryan as the man who managed to make you want to open up to love again!».

Rachele gave her an unconvinced look and didn't reply: she was tired and just wanted to go to bed.

They sat for a little longer, and then Anna, after hugging her and urging her to call if she needed anything, left.

That night, Rachele had a disturbing dream: she was in Ryan's room, on the terrace. In front of her stretched the stormy sea. She saw someone in the water—a man, drowning, overcome by the force of the storm.

Gripped by a sudden sense of terror, she realised that it was him, desperately screaming her name, hoping she might save him.

She woke up with a start, covered in sweat, her heart beating wildly.

Was it possible that he was really in danger? Was it possible that something horrible had happened to him that was preventing him from getting in touch with her? «I have to go back to Greece!», she murmured in the silence of the night.

She had no logical explanation, yet she knew it was the right thing to do.

She was sweating from head to toe, her heartbeat racing: that dream had caused her a sense of unease that lingered throughout the following day, until it led her to realise she really wanted to return to that place, even without a logical explanation.

A phrase she had read somewhere came to mind, even if she didn't remember from where:

"If a person doesn't look for you, it means they don't miss you and, if they don't miss you, they don't need you". Very true, she thought, even though she didn't care to attribute any particular meaning to those words. She needed that man and was willing to do anything to find him again, for she had realised that loving him meant touching his soul and being unable to live without him.

She would return to Greece.

Chapter Nine

To fight against great adversity, you need a lot of motivation, but also great courage... and a lot of character. What did Rachele possess? Nothing, yet everything. Nothing that could stimulate her, nothing that could motivate her, nothing that could encourage her— nothing that she could lose.

Yet, she felt she had everything she needed to face that new test: the desire to seek the truth, the need to find traces of the road that had led her to love again. Indeed, it was love that propelled her into that absurd search.

It was September 5 when she took off from Genoa, headed to the southern Peloponnese, feeling like a soldier about to face the mission of her life.

Only Marina knew where she was going; she had simply told the others that she would be away for a few days for a refresher course in Rome. She wanted to keep what she had in mind secret, as it was her business alone and no one else's.

Furthermore, she was ashamed of the rash decision she had made. Who could have understood her?

Going on a journey in search of a man with whom she had only spent a few days and with whom she hadn't even been able to communicate because of the language barrier; a man who had never called her and with whom she had fallen in love. Anyone would have laughed at her. No one could understand what those few days, that smile, those eyes, and that wonderful night had rekindled in her. «Just promise me you'll be careful», Marina had warned her.

Rachele had nodded, reassuringly: everything would be fine. She arrived in the evening and took a taxi that dropped her off in front of the hotel, not far from the one where Ryan had stayed. She had booked a nice room, with a sea view. After putting her luggage away, she decided to go out for something to eat.

Autumn was approaching, there were only a few people on the streets. "It's better like this", she thought to herself; she wasn't there to meet new people, she had come to Greece to look for information.

She had dinner in a half-empty place that nevertheless served excellent Greek food and, after drinking a horrible cup of coffee, went back to the hotel. Once in her room, she took a shower and then went to bed. Tiredness from the trip got the better of her and she fell asleep almost immediately.

The next morning at seven thirty she was already up, ready to begin her search. She had breakfast at the hotel bar, then took a walk on the beach to gather her thoughts and, when she felt ready, she set off towards Ryan's residence.

When she got to her destination, she plucked up some courage and rang the bell next to the glass door. She waited a few seconds, then, on the other side, the doorman arrived, an elderly man who stared at her curiously.

After a few moments, he opened.
When they were standing in front of each other, the man asked something that was probably in Greek. Seeing that she didn't understand, he switched to English. "Oh God, what do I do now?", Rachele said to herself, feverishly thinking of a solution. When she left, she hadn't even considered the fact that she would have great difficulty communicating. It was too late, now. «I don't understand... I'm from Italy», she muttered weakly in Italian.

The doorman raised his eyebrows.

«I'm looking for Ryan… Walsh», she then added, also in Italian, hoping the man would understand why she was there.

The man frowned, shook his head, then invited her to follow him towards the counter of the reception. Rachele thought that, more than a reception, it must have been the desk where he worked. There was a computer, which was switched off. A large register and a mailbox containing post. A telephone that seemed to have come straight from a seventies movie.

The man went behind the desk, picked up the receiver and dialled a three-digit number.

After a few moments, he began to speak quickly and the only word Rachele could understand was "Dafne". He ended the call and, with a polite gesture, pointed to a small sofa nearby.

Rachel, knowing she couldn't do otherwise, sat down. The doorman, who wore a calm expression and had a large white moustache that reminded her of her maternal grandfather, sat down in his armchair and, almost as if she weren't there, picked up a newspaper and began to read.

Rachele took out her cell phone: since she had arrived, she had only used it to send a text message to Marina the previous evening, to let her know that she had arrived and that she was fine.

As she was checking her phone, a sound caught her attention: it was the chime of the elevator door, from which she saw a small girl emerge, wearing the unmistakable attire of a cleaning lady. She had long black hair and eyes so dark that they were sharp. Looking at her more closely, she said to herself that she vaguely resembled Maria Callas.

The girl immediately went to the doorman. They exchanged a few words, then the man pointed to Rachele. She stared at her for a moment, then approached the sofa.

«Good morning, I'm Dafne», the girl introduced herself in almost flawless Italian, albeit with a strong Greek accent. «My father told me that you came here, but that you doesn't speak Greek or English… how can we help you?».

Rachele was astounded and couldn't have hoped for more. She stood up and, holding out her hand, introduced herself, then added: «This summer, in June, I was here in Kalamata…», she sighed.

«I met a man, Ryan Walsh, who was staying in this residence… we agreed that we would keep in contact with each other, but since I returned to Italy, I haven't heard from him… I came back here because I wanted to ask you if, by any chance… well, if he left an address… I'd really like to get in touch with him». Her pleading look softened Dafne's face and she immediately translated for her father.

He listened very carefully to what his daughter was saying, then a troubled expression shook his calm demeanour.

He spoke at length to Dafne in a sombre voice and she was unable to hide the distress, which Rachele immediately perceived.

«Is something wrong?», she asked, her heart pounding.

«My father said he knows who you're looking for… an Irishman, the owner of one of the apartments». She looked Rachele in the eyes. «He said that his sister came here at the end of July because…», then she hesitated. «Please tell me what happened!», Rachele begged, thinking back to the horrible dream in which Ryan drowned in the middle of a storm.

«Because her brother died shortly after returning to Dublin».

Rachele felt a pang in her chest, then everything around her went black.

A few moments later, she opened her eyes without remembering where she was. She saw two faces above hers: one of an old man and the other of a rather young girl. Their eyes were staring at her and conveyed great concern.

«She's recovering!», the girl said.

«How are you feeling? Do you need a doctor?». Rachele wondered what she was talking about for a moment, then suddenly remembered what had happened and that terrible discovery: Ryan was dead.

The man who had stolen her heart was no more. With tears in her eyes, she sat up, fighting a dizziness that almost made her fall back down.

«Are you okay?», Dafne asked again and she nodded: yes, she was physically fine, but everything else had fallen to pieces.

She tried to recover and in a thin voice asked the girl:

«Would it be possible to visit Ryan's apartment?». After hearing the translation, the doorman nodded and took the keys to the apartment. Rachele's eyes were a small sea of tears.

As soon as they entered, she felt a level of pain that she had never experienced before and that threatened to overwhelm her again. However, she steeled herself and, reassuring them that she was fine, asked if they could leave her alone for a few moments. Again, they obliged her and waited outside.

She found herself alone in that apartment and looked around, tears running down her face.

She saw the wonderful view from the large window of the living room and, for a few moments, she closed her eyes and imagined reliving the sweet night they had spent together. Their only night of love, which had enjoined them.

Her face in shock and streaked with tears, she left the apartment and asked the others if she could rent it for a few days.

The girl, moved by Rachele's pleading expression, translated that request to her father, almost begging him.

The two spoke for a moment, then Dafne turned to Rachele:

«He said okay, in fact, since you had a relationship with Mr Walsh, you can stay for free for a couple of days... the apartment is for sale and, since there are no planned visits from potential buyers, there aren't any problems, we'll take responsibility».

«The apartment has been put up for sale?», Rachele asked, dismayed.

«Yes, Mr Walsh's sister already has another property here in Kalamata».

For a moment, she considered whether to purchase that nest, where she had found happiness again, even though she knew it was an absurd idea, especially since an apartment like that must cost an arm and a leg.

She thanked Dafne and her father Nikolas for their help, understanding and compassion.

She went to get her things from the hotel and, within an hour, had moved into her new accommodation, without realising that, in so doing, she was voluntarily opening the doors of despair.

Succumbing to the pain, she began to speak to herself in a desperate voice, almost as if he were with her and could hear:

«I would have liked to get to know you better, I would have liked to caress your face again, I would have liked our world of emotions to have lasted longer... I would have liked to be better so that I might speak your language well, to be able to understand you and talk to you... I would have liked to savour your life and try to build a new one together. Now, it seems impossible to think of not loving you, even for just one day». Suddenly, she felt paralysed, bereft of any strength, drained of any stimulus.

The only feeling that remained was one of helplessness and the only certainty was that of having lost all hope. She didn't eat that evening, she fell asleep exhausted, hugging the pillow to protect herself from all that pain, tormenting herself over being there alone in that bed, where two and a half months before she had experienced that immense, unique passion, so to chase away the pain, she imagined she was still there in his arms. The next morning, at around eleven, while she was still in bed, Rachele heard the doorbell ring. With great difficulty, she went to the door: it was Dafne, holding a bag and a cup of hot coffee, with a reassuring smile.

«My father and I thought you might need this». The father and daughter had sensed Rachele's anguish and decided to take care of her, so she could get through that crisis.

«Thank you so much», she replied, struggling to get the words out.

Dafne said goodbye and then went back to her work. Since the pangs of hunger had already begun to make themselves felt, she drank the coffee and devoured the contents of the bag: a pita, a typical Greek flat bread with fresh tomato, olives and feta.

Buoyed by that precious snack, she sat up on the bed, thinking about what to do: she had discovered the truth and had become aware of how cruel fate had been. She found all that had happened terribly unfair and kept wondering why it had happened to her. She shook her head: there was no answer to that question. What she wanted at that moment was not to leave that apartment, indeed, she intended to stay there, for as long as possible.

In the afternoon, she called Dafne, gave her some money, and asked if she could buy her something to eat and drink for a couple of days. «Maybe it would be best if you went out... this isn't good...», the girl replied.

«I'm too sick to go out», Rachele replied, ending the matter. Both Nikolas and Dafne helped her because they understood the woman's state of mind.

They showered her with care and attention, but without being too intrusive. They brought her hearty breakfasts and, in the evening, for dinner, abundant portions of fish and desserts that, if nothing else, managed to make her feel better, at least for a while.

She stayed in that apartment for two very long days, crying and despairing, unable to accept that mocking fate.

She finally understood that it was pointless asking herself what the meaning of life was anymore, especially because the answer would never come if not from herself.

She began to become convinced that it was right to feel pain, but that it should in no way prevail over everything else, because that would have meant she would only be wasting precious time and, as those events had taught her, life had unpredictable turns and could end in an instant.

She spent two more days in that house, only going out for a walk by the sea in the early hours of the morning and late at night.

Fate had taken its course and she had a duty to herself to find the least painful way to process her loss. So, she decided to leave that place, even though she already had another goal in mind: go to Dublin to look for Ryan's sister and visit the place where he was buried. She wanted to say a last goodbye to that sweet, lovable man who had made her feel a kind of happiness she had never experienced before.

Before leaving, she asked Dafne and her father for a last favour: she asked for the name and address of Ryan's sister, then she hugged them both with great affection, thanking them infinitely for the warmth and understanding they had shown towards her.

«I will never forget this», she said, emotionally.

Then, Dafne and Rachele exchanged phone numbers so they could stay in touch, promising to see each other again and, in any event, so that she could tell them about her visit to Ryan's sister in Dublin.

She left for Italy with a tired, sad heart, but with a new goal that gave her the strength to look and forge forwards.

Once she returned home, she immediately went back to work.

Seeing her enter the office with swollen eyes and a sullen expression, Marina asked her if she was okay and begged her to tell her everything that had happened in Kalamata. Plucking up the courage, Rachele told her friend what she had learned and burst into tears, unable to hold back. Marina hugged her tightly, trying to console her; she told her to be strong and that time would heal her wounds.

«If you don't feel like it, forget about work... you can go home right now».

She shook her head, «No, if I stay without doing anything for another day, I risk going crazy». Marina, understanding her friend's state of mind, nodded, understanding that adding anything else would be superfluous.

When she recovered her physical and mental strength, she thought about who she could go to Dublin with, because she considered it unthinkable to take that trip on her own. In Greece, she had been very lucky to have met someone who spoke Italian; however, she didn't want to leave it to chance on a matter that was so close to her heart.

At first, she thought of asking Anna: she had met Ryan and had witnessed that brief love story, which had ended so dramatically. However, her friend spoke English, but not fluently and she feared that she might encounter some difficulties conversing with Ryan's sister. So, she thought of Patrizia, another dear friend who happened to be a language teacher.

They had met two years earlier, when Patrizia had approached Rachele about buying an apartment in Savona. A good friendship had developed between the two, so much so that they had started spending time with each other regularly. They had never travelled together, but Rachele told herself that there was always a first time for everything in life.

She called her and, without beating around the bush, told her that she needed to talk to her because she had a huge favour to ask of her.

They agreed to meet for an aperitif the next day, at a bar where they had already been in the past.

When they met, after greeting each other and ordering drinks, Rachele began the conversation from the end and, without mincing her words, asked her to accompany her on a weekend to Dublin. «Oh my goodness, Rachele, you've caught me completely off guard... when were you thinking of going?».

«I haven't decided yet, maybe we can agree on something based on our respective commitments». «Why have you decided to go to Dublin?», asked Patrizia who, although she didn't yet know the reason, had understood that it couldn't be just a holiday. Rachele took a sip of her aperitif and, trying not to crumble, told her the whole story, starting from the holiday in June and concluding with what she had discovered on her return to Greece.

«Rachele, I'm so sorry!», said Patrizia, emotionally. «Of course I'll accompany you, gladly! It's just a matter of deciding when».

The two women then considered the best time for both of them and finally agreed on early October.

«I'll pay for both our trips, of course», Rachele was keen to point out.

«No way! You make the bookings, then we'll each pay our share».

Rachele nodded, even though she had no intention of doing as her friend had suggested: paying for her trip seemed like the right thing to do for the enormous favour she was doing her.

«However ...», added Patrizia, «before we leave you'll have to start studying English... I'll give you lessons! Believe me, nowadays it's not possible to travel around the world without knowing this language».

She replied that she was absolutely right and that she would be more than happy to do so; then, she added that because she was too busy, she had always put it off, and on weekends she was too lazy and had other commitments, so she had always had some excuse for not taking a real English course.

In the weeks that followed, she threw herself into her work, intent on giving Marina as much rest as possible: she deserved it, since she herself had enjoyed far too many holidays and, more importantly, was planning to be away again.

In the meantime, she booked the flights and looked for a hotel in the same area where Ryan's sister lived. After a detailed search, she found one that offered breakfast at a reasonable price, so she booked a double room.

When she was done, she realised that everything was ready and that all that remained was to wait for the day of departure and thus face the harsh reality that awaited her in Dublin.

Finally, 4 October arrived and when she got on the plane, she got the feeling that the trip would force her to put something important behind her and that thence flight was taking her towards the conclusion of a short, yet intense part of her life that would never return. They landed at Dublin International Airport in the late afternoon and took a taxi to a hotel called "The Irish Joke". When they got out of the car, Rachele shivered: it was very cold compared to Italy and she couldn't wait to take a long, hot shower.

Ryan's sister lived about a kilometre from the hotel.

Rachele had Patrizia call her three days before leaving. She had explained the reason for the phone call and how Rachele had found out about her brother's death. She also told her that her dear friend wanted to visit Ryan's grave to say her last goodbyes.

The woman, who was moved by the story, replied that it would be a pleasure to accompany them and that all they had to do was call her as soon as they arrived in Ireland.

«Shall we call her now?», asked Patrizia, as she put her clothes away in the closet.

«Yes, that way we can make arrangements for tomorrow».

So, they phoned her and agreed to meet the next day, mid-morning, at a place near her house.

Shortly after, the two women left the hotel room to go to a place across the street to eat something. Then, they went back to rest.

The next morning, they took a taxi and headed to the *Dragonfly*, the agreed meeting place, where they found a tall, blonde woman waiting for them, her hair tied back at the nape of her neck. Her outfit was impeccable: dark green trousers and jacket and a cream-coloured shirt. After the formal introductions, Patrizia added that they were deeply saddened by her loss.

They entered the establishment, where they were welcomed by a warm, comfortable environment, where wood was the main feature. They sat around a small table and ordered a coffee. Meaghan was forty-five years old, she told the two women that she lived with Sam, her partner of three years. She worked in her brother's office and, since he died, she had been struggling to keep the business going with her partner and another collaborator.

Then, she talked about Ryan and Rachele soon realised she was unable to bear the conversation: hearing her talk about the man she had loved and dreamed of for months... it was heartbreaking to listen to her friend's translations, in which the sister emotionally described his life, his strength, his good and kind soul.

For her, everything had ended with that last kiss and the huge hug they had exchanged in Greece.

When it was obvious that Rachele was close to despair,

Meaghan took her hand and squeezed it gently, then suggested they not wait any longer and went to the place where he was buried to pay homage to him.

They got into the woman's car. The drive was quite short and, when Meaghan parked, Rachele was overcome by nervous anxiety, which she tried to control: too many emotions all at once risked making her crumble and she didn't want a repeat of what had happened in Kalamata, when she had fainted in front of Nikolas and Dafne. She took a couple of deep breaths, then from her purse she took a small red porcelain rose that she had bought for Ryan, a flower that would never wither, just like the love she felt for him.

They arrived at an open-air Irish cemetery: the tombstones seemed to come out of the ground and were neatly arranged in small gardens separated by concrete paths; in silence, Rachele and her friend followed Meaghan until she stopped in front of a grave. Rachele, trembling and still stressed by anxiety, drew closer.

With teary eyes, she looked at the photo of the man printed on the tombstone.

She looked at it for a long time, then turned to Patrizia and Meaghan, looked at the photo again and then at the two women again, lost.

«Are you okay?», Patrizia asked her, seeing her so confused.

«This man... isn't Ryan... I mean, he's not the Ryan I met in Greece...».

Patrizia, who was confused in turn, looked at Meaghan and stammered as she translated.

The three women looked at each other, astonished.

Clearing her throat and with more determination, Rachele repeated: «It's not the same man ... I tell you, it's not Ryan!».

Seized by a sudden dizziness, she clung to her friend, who held her up.

«Rachele, try to breathe deeply», she said, noticing she had turned pale, «take some deep breaths, then try to explain what you're saying!».

Rachele closed her eyes and breathed calmly and deeply, trying to slow down the beating of her heart, which was pounding like crazy, almost as if it was looking for a way out of her chest.

Meanwhile, Meaghan, who was stunned, kept looking from the photo to Rachele.

«Please explain what you're saying», Patrizia urged her gently, her tone nevertheless firm, so that she would understand that the time had come to shed light on the situation. Especially for Meaghan, who had been so kind and helpful.

So, after a couple more deep breaths, staring into the eyes of the two women, she began to speak: «Ryan Walsh... his photo, you know... it's not the same person I met in Greece... they're completely different», then she described the man she had met and who had changed her life in great detail.

Meaghan listened very carefully to Patrizia's translation, then mulled things over for a few minutes and unexpectedly put a hand to her mouth, her eyes widening in disbelief...

«Oh my God!», she exclaimed and began to speak quickly.

«Patrizia?», Rachele asked, hating the fact that she couldn't understand what the woman was saying, hating the cultural barrier that had suddenly come between her and the truth. She had started studying English seriously a few weeks earlier, but apart from a few simple sentences, she was unable to understand more complex ones.

Her friend turned to her and, with an expression of surprise, said: «She thinks you're talking about her brother's best friend, who was also his business partner... his name is Anfudan Ryan Lynch, but always introduces himself as Ryan because he doesn't like his first name». «My God», Rachele whispered, putting a hand on her heart, feeling an emotion so powerful that it almost made her lose touch with reality. So, her Ryan was alive!

She looked up at Meaghan: that dear woman had suffered a terrible loss and although she had only known her for a few hours, she felt a profound compassion for her. She went to her and gave her a big hug.

«I'm so sorry about your brother», she said with sincere emotion, «From the way you talked about him, even though I never met him, I understood that he was a beautiful person».

Patrizia obviously translated.

«Thank you», she replied, her voice trembling. Rachele placed the porcelain rose on the grave, said a prayer in a low voice, then, relieved with newfound hope, she left the cemetery, followed by the other two. Meaghan invited them to get into her car and during the journey that would take them to her house, she told them that her brother and Anfudan had worked together for fifteen years and had formed a formidable partnership; it was Anfudan, or rather the other Ryan, who mainly dealt with foreign affairs.

She continued her story: «In June, they were both in Greece... first in Kalamata, then my brother Ryan went to Athens to close a sale with Norwegian investors, while Anfudan stayed there to close another sale... it's amazing how fate sometimes plays with human beings», she said as she drove.

Rachele nodded; fate was sardonic, mischievous like a small child who enjoys tormenting others. However, she couldn't help but rejoice at that unexpected turn of events: after all, she thought she had lost him forever.

Now, however, everything was still up in the air.

Everything was still possible.

She closed her eyes and, with a faint smile, promised herself that she would now do everything in her power to find him again.

The story continued as they climbed the stairs to the apartment: Anfudan had been married for almost ten years, until his wife left him for a much younger guy with whom she had moved to Norway. He had a thirteen-year-old son, Michael, who he unfortunately saw very little because his mother had taken him with her.

«He suffered a lot», she concluded, as she opened the door, «but thanks to work and friends he managed to overcome that difficult period in his life».

Once home, the woman sat down at a desk and turned on the computer, with Rachele and Patrizia nearby. She fiddled with the keyboard for a few moments, until a photo appeared that occupied the entire computer screen. «That's him, right?», she asked, pointing to the face of the man Rachele was looking for.

«Yes!!! Yes, that's him!!», she said, realising she had almost shouted. There he was! It really was him! The man who had bewitched her.

So many emotions in the space of a few hours, ranging from desperation to the most intense joy, as if her heart had ended up on a roller coaster and she, who only wanted to find some emotional balance, wanted to get off as soon as possible.

Through Patrizia, Rachele timidly asked if it was possible to contact Ryan. She wanted to know where he was, ask him why he had never tried to get in touch with her and find out if he had forgotten her. She wanted to hear his voice again.

«I can tell you where he is», said Meaghan.

«A few days ago, he went to Croatia for work, then he will have to go back to Greece to meet a person who's interested in buying my brother's apartment, I can call him easily enough, but maybe we should wait until late afternoon, when he'll have finished work».

While waiting for the right moment to contact him, Meaghan asked about the story in which Rachele played such an important part.

The woman began telling her story, starting from the decision to go on holiday with two dear friends in Greece and concluding with her return to that place because she was driven by a dream in which she had glimpsed Ryan in danger and screaming her name; she continued talking about Nikolas and Dafne, who had revealed the man's death and she, shaken, begged the father and daughter to let her stay a couple of days in the apartment; she also mentioned that they had stayed by her side during those difficult days in which she was traumatised by the news of having lost the man who had made her find love once more.

«It was then that I decided to come here to Dublin, basically... to say a last goodbye».

«It's really incredible! You've shown great mental strength in every journey you've undertaken! You're driven by a very profound sentiment for a man you had known so little, but who had evidently already given you a lot, as you had probably given him», Meaghan said, squeezing her hand affectionately, «I'm sure my brother would have been happy... he really loved Anfudan, they were very close».

A tear fell silent and clear from her eyes.

Rachel, in a burst of sincere affection, gave her a big hug, feeling something that was very close to friendship towards Meaghan, as well as enormous gratitude. «Thank you for everything you're doing for me. I will never forget you and I will always pray for your brother».

They hugged again, this time even more tightly and that was one of the moments that Rachele would remember for the rest of her life. The warmth of that hug would remain forever in her heart.

Meaghan finally called Anfudan, while clarifying something important to Rachele:

«Never call him that... it's a name he can't stand. He says it's too old-fashioned and he's never liked it».

She smiled sweetly, then nodded, reassuring her that she had no intention of calling him that. For her, he was just Ryan.

«Actually, to tell the truth, I don't like that name, either!», Rachele confessed with a grimace. When the woman dialled the number, Rachele discovered that she was very upset again, tense, like the string of a violin. Now she had to get to the bottom of it all, it was the moment of truth and she was ready to accept anything that would follow, including rejection.

What really mattered was putting an end to this ordeal! The speakerphone was on; the phone was ringing and Rachele was restless... he answered after a few rings and, without giving him time to say a single word, Meaghan, remaining vague, informed him that there was a person who had come to Dublin especially for him. When Rachele heard him speak, she had to hold back a little cry of joy.

«Who's come to Dublin to see me?», he asked. As always, it was Patrizia who translated what they were saying for Rachele.

«I'll give you a hint…», Meaghan said with an ironic tone, "it's a woman».

«My God… it's not by any chance…»

«And she's from Italy», she quickly added before Ryan could make any reference to his ex-wife.

«From Italy?», he asked, perplexed, then… «It's not Rachele, by any chance?».

There was amazement in his voice and Rachele felt a shiver… he hadn't forgotten about her!

«Hi Ryan, how are you?», she greeted him, proudly showing off the few words she had learned in English. «Oh my God. …. Rachele!!!», he said in a voice that seemed broken by emotion, then he began to speak quickly, so much so that Meaghan stopped him, reminding him that the woman didn't speak English. «But there's a friend of hers who translates for her», she added.

Ryan replied something and Patrizia translated that he wanted to know how she had managed to find him.

Meaghan answered once again, telling him about the misunderstanding that had brought her all the way to Dublin.

The man remained silent for a few moments, then said that he was truly saddened by what had happened and by the suffering that Rachele had gone through. He added that he had tried to contact her several times and that the phone number she had left him was wrong and he hadn't been able to get in touch with her. She half-closed her eyes, calling herself stupid: that morning she had been in such a hurry to leave that she had even managed to write down her phone number incorrectly. A moment of carelessness that had cost her dearly!

«I even thought that you had given me the wrong number on purpose!».

«I never stopped thinking about you», Rachele replied in Italian, having it translated by Patrizia.

«Me too and I was very bitter about not being able to reach you. Then, my friend's death took away the joy I had just found with you. Thank you for fighting with all your strength for both of us. We couldn't lose sight of each other». At that point, he had an idea: «Why don't you join me in Kalamata? I have a business meeting there that will take longer than expected and I want to see you as soon as possible!».

Patrizia, with a sunny smile, translated for the umpteenth time and, without hesitation, Rachele said: «Yes! It's perfect!!», she said in English, then in Italian she added, «I just need to sort a couple of things out and I'll come and join you!».

They said goodbye affectionately, this time with the certainty of seeing each other again, and hung up. They spent the evening at Meaghan's house, who prepared a tasty dish of pancakes and potatoes called *Boxty potato* for her guests, all accompanied by the inevitable local beer.

For dessert, she served a fresh, delicate cake called *lemon and vanilla curd*.

A new friendship was born and the love, hope and joy of looking to the future with renewed optimism had returned. They stayed up talking until late, then Sam took them back to the hotel in his car.

That evening, after a long time, Rachele finally fell asleep peacefully and the anguish that had enveloped her for months like a second skin seemed to have vanished.

Chapter Ten

The following morning, they waited for Meaghan at the entrance of their hotel: the woman had offered to show them around the city.

When she arrived, Rachele and Patrizia got into the car and the first place she took them to was the Cathedral of St Patrick, the patron saint of Ireland, where the saint baptised the faithful at the famous bottomless well, and she told them that during his sermons, he used to explain to the faithful the concept of the Trinity using clover, which later became the symbol of Ireland.

They entered the church and, looking upwards, the two women were struck by the charm of the ancient organ, one of the largest in the country, boasting four thousand pipes.

Meaghan continued, saying that over five hundred tombs of illustrious people could be found there, mostly archbishops.

Afterwards, they took a short tour of the city by car and parked in the centre, in the historic cultural district of Dublin, for a walk along the characteristic cobbled streets, visiting numerous places.

Rachele particularly appreciated Temple Bar, a meeting place for street musicians, called Buskers, who, given the level of entertainment and quality of their performances, were on an equal footing with the great artists who were renowned throughout the world. They stopped to listen to a young man who, with his guitar, played the acoustic version of "Fast car" by Tracy Chapman.

At the end, when he had finished, all three women applauded the artist, leaving a few pounds in his musical instrument case.

«Have a beer on me!», Rachele said, through Patrizia. The boy smiled sweetly and replied that he would toast in honour of the beautiful woman who had been so kind. Lastly, they took a drive to see Dublin Castle from the outside, a fortress located on the southern bank of the River Liffey. They admired the circular tower, known as the Record Tower and Meaghan revealed that it was the only building of the ancient Norman fortresses that was still standing.

They then stopped to eat something at a characteristic establishment.

On Meaghan's advice, Rachele chose *corned beef*, a stew in a crust, while Patrizia had a sliced steak of clack angus with potatoes. Meaghan chose a hamburger with spicy potatoes, whereas, for dessert, they ordered apple fritters. They found everything delicious. Before returning to the hotel, they passed a stately building surrounded by trees and a well-kept garden and Meaghan explained to the two women that Ryan lived there. Surprised to find herself in that very place, Rachele was fascinated by the building and imagined the everyday life of the man she had fallen in love with. Since it had become evening, they returned to the hotel and, before parting, they exchanged contact details and promises of hospitality. Meaghan wished Rachele good luck and to be happy with Ryan, then promised the two women that they would undoubtedly see each other again in the near future.

Rachele responded with a strong, emotional hug, full of gratitude for the woman, who had recently suffered such a great loss and who, without even knowing them, offered them help and deep hospitality.

When they returned to the hotel, Rachele and Patrizia were very tired, but satisfied with having spent the day in the company of a new friend, which had allowed them to enjoy the sights of Dublin.

The next day, they went to the airport and arrived in Savona in late morning; without even unpacking her suitcase, Rachele went straight to the office: she couldn't wait to tell Marina about her incredible adventure. Her friend was particularly struck by the tale: «If it had happened to someone else, I'd have had a hard time believing it! So, in short... in the end it was all just a gigantic misunderstanding!».

«Yes, a misunderstanding that nevertheless allowed me to find Ryan again!».

Marina nodded, singing her friend's praises: «I've always admired your determination, you're a woman who doesn't give up in the face of adversity, doesn't stop at appearances and never settles for less, you know what you want and your intuition has almost always steered you right. Don't waste any more time and hurry towards the happiness you've earned yourself!!». Over the following days, Rachele devoted herself completely to her work: Marina deserved a break and, indeed, she took advantage of it to enjoy a little vacation at a wellness spa.

Every evening that week at the end of October, Patrizia went to Rachele's house to continue her English lessons. She would arrive promptly at seven o'clock, they studied for about two hours, then after dinner they resumed their lessons with the utmost commitment. Patrizia wanted to teach her at least the basics of the language, enough to allow her friend to exchange a few words with Ryan.

Obviously, that was only the beginning of a long path. «You'll have all the time in the world to perfect the language... right now you only need the bare essentials, you'll have other things to do anyway...!», she said, winking at her mischievously.

It was thanks to those lessons that Rachele began to write short messages to Ryan. Every evening, before wishing each other goodnight, he would ask her when she would go and visit him.

Rachele deliberately didn't reveal the day of her arrival: she wanted to surprise him.

A few days later, she arrived at Kalamata airport, where she took a taxi; before getting to his place, she asked the taxi driver, a skinny, good-natured guy, to stop along the way to buy a bottle of champagne.

When the intercom rang, Nikolas came out to welcome her, followed by Dafne. They hugged each other emotionally. Rachele was about to tell them what had happened, but the doorman already knew everything because, in the meantime, he had spoken to Ryan.

«I'm sorry I caused you so much pain!», he apologised, translated by Dafne, who tried to express the regret and guilt her father felt.

«Oh no, I just have to thank you! If it weren't for you, I would never have found the real Ryan!», she replied, hugging him again to reassure him.

They said goodbye and she headed towards the door of the apartment where she had felt so much happiness and then despair. Now, everything was different and everything had to be rebuilt.

She knocked on the door with the bottle of champagne in her hand.

He opened the door and, when he saw her, a mixture of disbelief and joy lit up his face; he radiated a profound sense of emotion.

They both remained silent, looking at each other from head to toe, stunned by the emotion of having finally found each other again. Then, he let her in and, without giving her time to say a single word, he took the bottle from her hands, which he placed on the cabinet in the entrance, then held her tightly.

He closed the door with one foot, gently laid her on the sofa and smothered her in kisses.

It was an overwhelming, magical encounter, which had been desired for too long; their lips were joined once more and neither of them could or wanted to escape the other.

Everything they needed was in their hearts and was merely waiting to come to the light like a flower whose roots had just one name: love.

Day broke and when the alarm rang, calling Ryan back to work, neither of them left the bed, unable to leave each other.

«I'm staying with you today», Ryan said with a smile and, reaching for his mobile phone, he informed his client that they couldn't meet that day due to an unexpected event. He apologised, postponing everything until the next day.

«Fantastic!», Rachele said, pulling him closer and discovering that she couldn't get enough of him. She had never felt so overwhelmed by such an intense desire for a man. With Ryan, everything was new and wonderful; she prayed that it would never end, that they wouldn't lose contact with each other again, for any reason.

"It won't happen", she said to herself, confident in herself and her feelings. "I'd even be prepared to go and live in Dublin…"; her thoughts flowed quickly, like torrents.

She really meant it! It wasn't an objective dictated by passion or the intensity of the moment. She would have followed him to the ends of the earth, leaving everything behind because she had understood, firsthand, that only love gave life meaning and made it worth living. In late morning, they heard the doorbell ring and Ryan, staggering, headed towards the door.

He opened it… but there was no one there, except for a trolley covered by a tablecloth.

He looked around curiously, lifted the cloth and discovered a large breakfast accompanied by a note. He returned to the room and, when Rachele saw it, she already imagined who could have been so thoughtful. Ryan read the note written in English: - A little thought for two people in love. Be happy, Nikolas and Dafne. -

«Two really kind people», Rachele commented out loud, emotionally, thinking about how she might repay them for so much affection. She picked up her mobile phone and used a translation app to write out a sentence in English for Ryan: «Before we leave, we should get them a gift».

He completely agreed.

Since their energy levels were running low, they ate heartily, enjoying the good coffee, fresh fruit and more. When they had finished breakfast, they decided to go out; they went to greet and thank the doorman, who replied that it was just a small gift for two people who had been through a lot.

Rachele invited him and Dafne out to dinner.

Nikolas was hesitant, but then, faced with their insistence, gladly accepted.

«See you tonight, then!», Rachele said, walking towards the glass door of the residence.

«See you tonight!», Nikolas confirmed, smiling, as he returned to his desk.

They went outside, hand in hand, walking towards the promenade by the sea, kissed by the sun and lulled by a light wind that seemed to push them towards the future that was waiting for them.

Rachele looked at Ryan and wrapped herself in his embrace as they walked towards the beach.

The End

DID THIS STORY TOUCH YOUR HEART?
Join **Daniela Di Domenico's Readers Circle** *and be the first to know when the next tale of secrets and passion arrives.*

Scan the QR code to stay in touch.